PRINCE RABBIT
and
THE PRINCESS WHO
COULD NOT LAUGH

PRINCE RABBIT *and*

With illustrations in full color by Mary Shepard

THE PRINCESS WHO COULD NOT LAUGH

by A. A. Milne

E. P. Dutton & Company, Inc., New York

PRINCE RABBIT

Once upon a time there was a King who had no children. Sometimes he would say to the Queen, 'If only we had a son!' and the Queen would answer, 'If only we had!' And then on another day he would say, 'If only we had a daughter!' and the Queen would sigh and answer, 'Yes, even if we had a daughter, that would be something!' But they had no children at all.

As the years went on and there were still no children in the Royal Palace, the people began to ask each other who would be the next King to reign over them. And some said that perhaps it would be the Chancellor, which was a pity, as nobody liked him very much; and others said that there would be no King at all, but that everybody would be equal. Those who were lowest of all thought that this would be a satisfactory ending of the matter; but those who were higher up felt that, though in some respects it would be a good thing, yet in other respects it would be an ill-advised state of affairs; and they hoped therefore that a young Prince would be born in the Palace. But no Prince was born.

One day, when the Chancellor was in audience with the King, it seemed well to him to speak what was in the people's minds.

'Your Majesty,' he said; and then stopped, wondering how best to put it.

'Well?' said the King.

'I have Your Majesty's permission to speak my mind?'

'So far, yes,' said the King.

Encouraged by this, the Chancellor resolved to put the matter plainly.

'In the event of Your Majesty's death . . .' He coughed and began again. 'If Your Majesty ever should die,' he said, 'which in any case will not be for many years—if ever—as, I need hardly say, Your Majesty's loyal subjects earnestly hope—I mean they hope it will be never. But assuming for the moment—making the sad assumption—'

'You said you wanted to speak your mind,' interrupted the King. 'Is this it?'

'Yes, Your Majesty.'

'Then I don't think much of it.'

'Thank you, Your Majesty.'

'What you are trying to say is, "Who will be the next King?"'

'Quite so, Your Majesty.'

'Ah!' The King was silent for a little. Then he said, 'I can tell you who won't be.'

The Chancellor did not seek for information on this

point, feeling that in the circumstances the answer was obvious.

'What do you suggest yourself?'

'That Your Majesty choose a successor from among the young and the highly-born of the country, putting him to whatever test seems good to Your Majesty.'

The King pulled at his beard and frowned.

'There must be not one test, but many tests. Let all, who will, offer themselves, provided only that they are under the age of twenty and are well-born. See to it.'

He waved his hand in dismissal, and with an accuracy established by long practice the Chancellor retired backwards out of the Palace.

On the following morning, therefore, it was announced that all those who were ambitious to be appointed the King's successor, and who were of high birth and not yet come to the age of twenty, should present themselves a week later for the tests to which His Majesty desired to put them, the first of which was to be a running race. Whereat the people rejoiced, for they wished to be ruled by one to whom they could look up, and running was much esteemed in that country.

On the appointed day the excitement was great. All along the course, which was once round the Palace, large crowds were massed, and at the finishing point the King and Queen themselves were seated in a specially erected Pavilion. And to this Pavilion the competitors were brought to be introduced to Their Majesties. And there were nine young nobles, well-built and handsome, and (it was thought) intelligent, who were competitors.

And there was also one Rabbit.

The Chancellor had first noticed the Rabbit when he

was lining up the competitors, pinning numbers on their backs so that the people should identify them, and giving them such instructions as seemed necessary to him.

'Now, now, be off with you,' he had said. 'Competitors only, this way.' And he had made a motion of impatient dismissal with his foot.

'I am a competitor,' said the Rabbit. 'And I don't think it is usual,' he added with dignity, 'for the starter to kick one of the competitors just at the beginning of an important foot-race. It looks like favouritism.'

'You can't be a competitor,' laughed all the young nobles.

'Why not? Read the rules.'

The Chancellor, feeling rather hot suddenly, read the rules. The Rabbit was certainly under twenty; he had a pedigree which showed that he was of the highest birth; and—

'And,' said the Rabbit, 'I am ambitious to be appointed the King's successor. Those were all the conditions. Now let's get on with the race.'

But first came the introduction to the King. One by one the competitors came up . . . and at the end—

'This,' said the Chancellor, as airily as he could, 'is Rabbit.' Rabbit bowed in the most graceful manner possible; first to the King and then to the Queen. But the King only stared at him. Then he turned to the Chancellor.

'Well?'

The Chancellor shrugged his shoulders.

'His entry does not appear to lack validity,' he said.

'He means, Your Majesty, that it is all right,' explained Rabbit.

The King laughed suddenly. 'Go on,' he said. 'We can

always have a race for a new Chancellor afterwards.'

So the race was started. And the young Lord Calomel was much cheered on coming in second; not only by Their Majesties, but also by Rabbit, who had finished the course some time before, and was now lounging in the Royal Pavilion.

'A very good style, Your Majesty,' said Rabbit, turning

to the King. 'Altogether he seems to be a most promising youth.'

'Most,' said the King grimly. 'So much so that I do not propose to trouble the rest of the competitors. The next test shall take place between you and him.'

'Not racing again, please, Your Majesty. That would hardly be fair to his Lordship.'

'No, not racing. Fighting.'

'Ah!' What sort of fighting?'

'With swords,' said the King.

'I am a little rusty with swords, but I daresay in a day or two—'

'It will be now,' said the King.

'You mean, Your Majesty, as soon as Lord Calomel has recovered his breath?'

The King answered nothing, but · turned to his Chancellor.

'Tell the young Lord Calomel that in half an hour I desire him to fight with this Rabbit—'

'The young Lord Rabbit,' murmured the other competitor to the Chancellor.

'To fight with him for my Kingdom.'

'And borrow me a sword, will you?' said Rabbit. 'Quite a small one. I don't want to hurt him.'

So, half an hour later, on a level patch of grass in front of the Pavilion, the fight began. It was a short, but exciting struggle. Calomel, whirling his long sword in his strong right arm, dashed upon Rabbit, and Rabbit, carrying his short sword in his teeth, dodged between Calomel's legs and brought him toppling. And when it was seen that the young Lord rose from the ground with a broken arm, and

that with the utmost gallantry he had now taken his sword in his left hand, the people cheered. And Rabbit, dropping his sword for a moment, cheered too; then he picked it up and got entangled in his adversary's legs again, so that again the young Lord Calomel crashed to the ground, this time with a sprained ankle. And there he lay.

Rabbit trotted to the Royal Pavilion, and dropped his sword in the Chancellor's lap.

'Thank you so much,' he said. 'Have I won?'

And the King frowned and pulled at his beard.

'There are other tests,' he muttered.

But what were they to be? It was plain that Lord Calomel was in no condition for another physical test. What, then, of an intellectual test?

'After all,' said the King to the Queen that night, 'intelligence is a quality not without value to a ruler.'

'Is it?' asked the Queen doubtfully.

'I have found it so,' said the King, a little haughtily.

'Oh,' said the Queen.

'There is a riddle, of which my father was fond, the answer to which has never been revealed save to the Royal House. We might make this the final test between them.'

'What is the riddle?'

'I fancy it goes like this.' He thought for a moment, and then recited it, beating time with his hand.

'My first I do for your delight.

Although 'tis neither black nor white.

My second looks the other way,

Yet always goes to bed by day.

My whole can fly, and climb a tree,

And sometimes swims upon the sea.'

'What is the answer?' asked the Queen.

'As far as I remember,' said His Majesty, 'it is either "dormouse" or "raspberry."'

'"Dormouse" doesn't make sense,' objected the Queen.

'Neither does "raspberry",' pointed out the King.

'Then how can they guess it?'

'They can't. But my idea is that young Calomel should be secretly told beforehand what the answer is, so that he may win the competition.'

'Is that fair?' asked the Queen doubtfully.

'Yes,' said the King. 'Certainly, or I wouldn't have suggested it.'

So it was duly announced by the Chancellor that the

final test between the young Lord Calomel and Rabbit would be the solving of an ancient riddle-me-ree, which in the past had baffled all save those of Royal Blood. Copies of the riddle had been sent to the competitors, and in a week from that day they would be called upon to give their answers before Their Majesties and the full Court. And with Lord Calomel's copy went a message, which said this:

'From a friend. The answer is "dormouse". BURN THIS.'

The day came round; and Calomel and Rabbit were brought before Their Majesties; and they bowed to Their Majesties, and were ordered to be seated, for Calomel's ankle was still painful to him. And when the Chancellor had called for silence, the King addressed those present, explaining the conditions of the test to them.

'And the answer to the riddle,' he said, 'is in this sealed paper, which I now hand to my Chancellor, in order that he shall open it, as soon as the competitors have told us what they know of the matter.'

The people, being uncertain what else to do, cheered slightly.

'I will ask Lord Calomel first,' His Majesty went on. He looked at his Lordship, and his Lordship nodded slightly. And Rabbit, noticing that nod, smiled suddenly to himself.

'Lord Calomel,' said the King, 'what do you consider to be the best answer to this riddle-me-ree?'

The young Lord Calomel tried to look very wise, and he said:

'There are many possible answers to this riddle-me-ree, but the best answer seems to me to be "dormouse".'

'Let someone take a note of that answer,' said the King;

whereupon the Chief Secretary wrote down: 'Lord Calomel—"dormouse".'

'Now,' said the King to Rabbit, 'what suggestion have you to make in this matter?'

Rabbit, who had spent an anxious week inventing

23

answers each more impossible than the last, looked down modestly.

'Well?' said the King.

'Your Majesty,' said Rabbit with some apparent hesitation, 'I have a great respect for the intelligence of the young Lord Calomel, but I think that in this matter he is mistaken. The answer is not, as he suggests, "woodlouse", but "dormouse".'

'I said "dormouse",' cried Calomel indignantly.

'I thought you said "woodlouse",' said Rabbit in surprise.

'He certainly said "dormouse",' said the King coldly.

'"Woodlouse", I think,' said Rabbit.

'Lord Calomel—"dormouse",' read out the Chief Secretary.

'There you are,' said Calomel, 'I did say "dormouse".'

'My apologies,' said Rabbit, with a bow. 'Then we are both right, for "dormouse" it certainly is.'

The Chancellor broke open the sealed paper, and to the amazement of nearly all present read out, "dormouse".'

'Apparently, Your Majesty,' he said in some surprise, 'they are both equally correct.'

The King scowled. In some way which he didn't quite understand, he had been tricked.

'May I suggest, Your Majesty,' the Chancellor went on, 'that they be asked now some question of a different order, such as can be answered, after not more than a few minutes' thought, here in Your Majesty's presence. Some problem in the higher mathematics for instance, such as might be profitable for a future King to know.'

'What question?' asked His Majesty, a little nervously.

'Well, as an example—"What is seven times six?"' And, behind his hand, he whispered to the King, 'Forty-two.' Not a muscle of the King's face moved, but he looked thoughtfully at the Lord Calomel. Supposing his Lordship did not know.

'Well?' he said reluctantly. 'What is the answer?'

The young Lord Calomel thought for some time, and then said, 'Fifty-four.'

'And you?' said the King to Rabbit.

Rabbit wondered what to say. As long as he gave the same answers as Calomel, he could not lose in the encounter, yet in this case 'forty-two' was the right answer. But the King, who could do no wrong, even in arithmetic, might decide, for the purposes of the competition, that 'fifty-four' was an answer more becoming to the future ruler of the country. Was it, then, safe to say, 'forty-two'?

'Your Majesty,' he said, 'there are several possible answers to this extraordinarily novel conundrum. At first sight the obvious solution would appear to be "forty-two". The objection to this solution is that it lacks originality. I have long felt that a progressive country such as ours might well strike out a new line in the matter. Let us

agree that in future seven sixes are "fifty-four". In that case the answer, as Lord Calomel has pointed out, is "fifty-four". But if Your Majesty would prefer to cling to the old style of counting, then Your Majesty and Your Majesty's Chancellor would make the answer "forty-two".'

After saying which, Rabbit bowed gracefully, both to Their Majesties and to his opponent, and sat down again.

The King scratched his head in a puzzled sort of way.

'The correct answer,' he said, 'is, or will be in the future, "fifty-four".'

'Make a note of that,' whispered the Chancellor to the Chief Secretary.

'Lord Calomel guessed this at his first attempt; Rabbit at his second attempt. I therefore declare Lord Calomel the winner.'

'Shame!' said Rabbit.

'Who said that?' cried the King furiously. Rabbit looked over his shoulder, with the object of identifying the culprit, but was apparently unsuccessful.

'However,' went on the King, 'in order that there should be no doubt in the minds of my people as to the absolute fairness with which this competition is being conducted, there will be one further test. It happens that a King is often called upon to make speeches and exhortations to his people, and for this purpose the ability to stand evenly upon two legs for a considerable length of time is of much value to him. The next test, therefore, will be—'

But at this point Lord Calomel cleared his throat so loudly that the King had to stop and listen to him.

'Quite so,' said the King. 'The next test, therefore, will be held in a month's time, when his Lordship's ankle is healed, and it will be a test to see who can balance himself longest upon two legs only.'

Rabbit lolloped back to his home in the wood, pondering deeply.

Now there was an enchanter who lived in the wood, a man of many magical gifts. He could (it was averred by the countryside) extract coloured ribbons from his mouth, cook plum-puddings in a hat, and produce as many as ten silk handkerchiefs, knotted together, from a twist of paper. And that night, after a simple dinner of salad, Rabbit called upon him.

'Can you,' he said, 'turn a rabbit into a man?'

'I can,' he said at last, 'turn a plum-pudding into a rabbit.'

'That,' said Rabbit, 'to be quite frank, would not be a helpful operation.'

'I can turn almost anything into a rabbit,' said the enchanter with growing enthusiasm. 'In fact, I like doing it.'

Then Rabbit had an idea.

'Can you turn a man into a rabbit?'

'I did once. At least I turned a baby into a baby rabbit.'

'When was that?'

'Eighteen years ago. At the court of King Nicodemus. I was giving an exhibition of my powers to him and his good Queen. I asked one of the company to lend me a baby, never thinking for a moment that . . . The young Prince was handed up. I put a red silk handkerchief over him, and waved my hands. Then I took the handkerchief

away . . . The Queen was very much distressed. I tried everything I could, but it was useless. The King was most generous about it. He said that I could keep the rabbit. I carried it about with me for some weeks, but one day it escaped. Dear, dear!' He wiped his eyes gently with a red silk handkerchief.

'Most interesting,' said Rabbit. 'Well, this is what I want you to do.' And they discussed the matter from the beginning.

A month later the great Standing Competition was to take place. When all was ready, the King rose to make his opening remarks.

'We are now,' he began, 'to make one of the most interesting tests between our two candidates for the throne. At the word "Go!" they will—' And then he stopped. 'Why what's this?' he said, putting on his spectacles. 'Where is the young Lord Calomel? And what is that second rabbit doing? There was no need to bring your brother,' he added severely to Rabbit.

'I am Lord Calomel,' said the second rabbit meekly.

'Oh!' said the King.

'Go!' said the Chancellor, who was a little deaf.

Rabbit, who had been practising for a month, jumped on his back paws and remained there. Lord Calomel, who had had no practice at all, remained on all fours. In the crowd at the back the enchanter chuckled to himself.

'How long do I stay like this?' asked Rabbit.

'This is all very awkward and distressing,' said the King.

'May I get down?' said Rabbit.

'There is no doubt that the Rabbit has won,' said the Chancellor.

'Which rabbit?' cried the King crossly. 'They're both rabbits.'

'The one with the white spots behind the ears,' said Rabbit helpfully. 'May I get down?'

There was a sudden cry from the back of the hall.

'Your Majesty!'

'Well, well, what is it?'

The enchanter pushed his way forward.

'May I look, Your Majesty?' he said in a trembling voice. 'White spots behind the ears? Dear, dear! Allow me!'

He seized Rabbit's ears and bent them this way and that.

'Ow!' said Rabbit.

'It is! Your Majesty, it is!'

'Is what?'

'The son of the late King Nicodemus, whose country is now joined to your own. Prince Silvio.'

'Quite so,' said Rabbit airily, hiding his surprise. 'Didn't any of you recognize me?'

'Nicodemus had only one son,' said the Chancellor, 'and he died as a baby.'

'Not died,' said the enchanter, and forthwith explained the whole sad story.

'I see,' said the King, when the story was ended. 'But of course that is neither here nor there. A competition like this must be conducted with absolute impartiality.' He turned to the Chancellor. 'Which of them won that last test?'

'Prince Silvio,' said the Chancellor.

'Then my dear Prince Silvio—'

'One moment,' interrupted the enchanter excitedly. 'I've just thought of the word. I knew there were some words you had to say'. He threw his red silk handkerchief over Rabbit, and cried, 'Hey presto!' And the handkerchief rose and rose and rose . . .

And there was Prince Silvio!

You can imagine how loudly the people cheered. But the King appeared not to notice that anything surprising had happened.

'Then, my dear Prince Silvio,' he went on, 'as the winner of this most interesting series of contests, you are appointed successor to our throne.'

'Your Majesty,' said Silvio, 'this is too much!' And he turned to the enchanter and said, 'May I borrow your handkerchief for a moment? My emotion has overcome me!'

So on the following day, Prince Rabbit was duly proclaimed heir to the throne before all the people. But not until the ceremony was over did he return the enchanter's handkerchief.

'And now,' he said to the enchanter, 'you may restore Lord Calomel to his proper shape.'

And the enchanter placed his handkerchief on Lord Calomel's head, and said, 'Hey presto!' and Lord Calomel stretched himself and said, 'Thanks very much!' But he said it rather coldly, as if he were not really very grateful.

So they all lived happily for a long time. And Prince Rabbit married the most beautiful Princess of those parts;

and when a son was born to them there was much feasting and jollification. And the King gave a great party, whereat minstrels, tumblers, jugglers and suchlike were present in large quantities to give pleasure to the company. But in spite of a suggestion made by the Princess, the enchanter was not present.

'But I hear he is so clever,' said the Princess to her husband.

'He has many amusing inventions,' replied the Prince, 'but some of them are not in the best of taste.'

'Very well, dear,' said the Princess.

THE PRINCESS WHO COULD NOT LAUGH

There was once a King who had an only daughter, the pride of his heart. She was sweet, she was good, she was beautiful, and the King would have said that she was perfection itself, but for one thing. She never laughed. Nothing seemed to amuse her.

Her father, the King, was often amused. The Court Fool had only to open his mouth, and His Majesty was leaning back in his throne roaring with laughter. Nobody was so quick as His Majesty to see the point of a good story or a clever riddle. But the Princess would listen gravely, and then say 'Fancy' or 'Did he really?' or 'Well, what happened next?' when the end of the joke had been reached. 'My darling,' the King would say, wiping away the tears of laughter which had come into his eyes, 'don't you understand? It's a joke!' And the Princess would answer, 'Yes I see it's a joke, Father, but why do you make that noise about it?'

For Her Royal Highness always said that she saw a joke as well as anybody. What made her different from the King was that when His Majesty saw a joke he had to make a loud roaring noise, whereas when she saw one, she didn't want to make any noise at all. Did that matter very much?

'My darling,' said the King, 'it isn't a question of wanting to. If you have a sense of humour, you have to laugh.'

'I don't,' said the Princess.

'I know,' sighed the King; 'you don't.'

And this made him very miserable. Nothing is so pleasant as to tell a funny story to somebody whom you love, to watch the smile coming on her face, and to hear her sudden laughter, and then to linger with her, your laughter catching new life from hers, in happy enjoyment of the joke. And this pleasure the King did not have.

He did his best. He read straight through to her, from beginning to end, that amusing book *One Thousand Merrie*

Jestes collected from Manye Sources, pausing for a moment at the end of each story so that her laughter should not run over on to the next story. But she never laughed once. He then read it through again; still she did not laugh. He

gave her to read for herself, *Diverting Tales from Divers Lands*, and watched her face anxiously. She did not smile.

Nothing that he could say or do, nothing that the Court Fool could say or do, changed the gravity of her face. She was sweet, she was good, she was beautiful—but she could not laugh.

A time came when the King could not bear it any longer, and he felt that somehow or other the young Princess must be moved to laughter. In his difficulty he consulted his Chancellor, than whom there was supposed to be no wiser man in His Majesty's Kingdom. Now the Chancellor had a son, the young Count Hoppo, a fellow of no great learning, nor beauty, nor bravery, a fellow indeed, of no personal attraction whatsoever, but a young man esteemed in his family as a jester. The Chancellor therefore spoke as follows:

'I would suggest Your Majesty, that it be announced to Your Majesty's faithful people that he who is the first able to move Her Royal Highness to laughter be rewarded by the hand of Her Royal Highness and half Your Majesty's Kingdom.'

'What do you say, my love?' said the King to his daughter.

'As you please,' said the Princess. 'I shall not laugh, for it seems that I have no wish to laugh, nor do I greatly desire to marry, but as you please.'

The King turned to his Chancellor.

'Let it be so announced,' he commanded. 'At noon henceforward, for the space of one half-hour, those with humorous riddles or merry jests to tell shall have audience before the whole Court, and he who first moves Her Royal Highness to laughter shall be rewarded by her hand in marriage.'

'And half the Kingdom?' said the Chancellor anxiously.

'Is that usual?' asked the King.

'Entirely, Your Majesty.'

'Very well. So be it. Tomorrow at noon we shall await the competitors.'

At noon, then, all those with good stories to tell or merry riddles to propound, attended at the Palace, and foremost amongst them was the young Count Hoppo. So one by one they put their riddles or told their stories, and Her Royal Highness listened to them.

'Tell me, Your Royal Highness,' said Count Hoppo, 'why does a dragon cross the road?'

The King, who knew this one, began to chuckle to himself.

'I suppose,' said the Princess, 'that he crosses the road in order to get to the other side.'

'Y-yes,' said Hoppo, a little annoyed. 'Yes, exactly.'

'Well?' said the Princess.

'That's all,' said Hoppo crossly.

'Was it funny?' she said, turning to the King.

'My dear,' said her father, 'you missed the point of the joke. The point of the joke was that if you said—I mean, what he expected you to say—then he would have said—only you didn't.'

'But why else should a dragon cross the road?'

'Quite so,' said the King quickly. 'Next competitor.'

Another young man stepped forward and enquired of Her Royal Highness why a silver bowl was like a wasp's nest.

'It isn't,' said the Princess. She turned to the King.

'Is it, Father?'

'It's a riddle, dear,' explained His Majesty, and he murmured to himself, 'why is a silver bowl like a wasp's nest—like a wasp's nest.'

'I still think it isn't,' said the Princess.

'Well?' said the King to the questioner. 'Why is a silver bowl like a wasp's nest?'

'Because there's a *B* in *both*, Your Majesty.'

His Majesty roared with laughter.

'Not in a wasp's nest,' said the Princess, 'surely!'

The King explained that the letter 'B' was in the word 'Both'.

'Then why drag in the wasp's nest?'

The King explained that that was the joke.

'I see,' said the Princess, but she did not laugh.

Then a third young man came forward, and this was the Count Rollo. Tall and handsome he was, and of a pleasant smiling countenance, so that the Princess thought to herself: 'If only he would win, and not that horrid Count Hoppo.'

Count Rollo, it seemed, desired to know the difference between a fly and a bird.

'A fly and a bird,' murmured the King to himself, 'a fly and a bird, a fly and a bird, a fly and a bird.'

The Princess hastened to tell him.

'A bird,' she said, 'has feathers on his wings, but a fly has not. A bird lays eggs, and a fly—no, that's wrong, because flies do lay eggs. But a fly hasn't got a beak. And it doesn't build a nest. Oh, and it's much smaller than a bird.'

'All this is true!' smiled Rollo, 'but there is another

difference, Your Royal Highness.'

'Well?' said the King.

'A bird can fly, Your Majesty, but a fly cannot bird.'

'Ha-ha-ha,' went the King. 'Ha-ha-ha-ha-ha. Ha-ha.'

'Cannot what?' asked the Princess.

'Cannot bird, Your Royal Highness.'

'But what is, "birding"?'

'That is what the poor fly never knew, Your Royal Highness, and often wondered. It seems so unfair, does it not, that if a bird can fly whenever it likes, the fly can never bird, however much it wants to.'

'It does seem rather unfair,' said the Princess, nodding to him in a friendly way.

But she did not laugh.

So, in their turn, all the young men of the country put their riddles and told their stories, not only on that day, but on many other days. And one by one, they grew tired of trying to make laugh a Princess who could not laugh, and they came no more to the Court at the hour of noon. But Count Hoppo and Count Rollo came always, for that Hoppo wished mightily for the half of His Majesty's Kingdom, and Rollo loved and was loved by the Princess.

So in the end they two stood there alone.

Now this was to be the last trial between them, wherefore each had spent the night in anxious preparation for the morrow, Rollo wondering which of the few stories he had left untold would be most likely to amuse the Princess and Hoppo bethinking him of a plan whereby at the same time he might win the Princess and discomfort his rival.

On the morrow, then, before the whole Court, Count Hoppo and Count Rollo made final trial for the hand of the Princess. And the Princess looked at them as they stood

there before her, and wished with all her heart that it might be Count Rollo who should make her laugh. So Count Rollo came forward to tell her his story.

'There was,' he said, 'a stranger who came into a far country, and he desired to know the way to the King's Palace, for he had a present to lay before the King. So he stopped one whom he met on the road and said to him: "Pray sir, do you know the way to the King's Palace?" Whereupon the man, wishing to be thought humorous, replied, "Yes I do," and walked on. But a moment later, fearing lest his joke should be mistaken for rudeness, he hurried after the stranger, and said, "I beg your pardon, sir, but do you wish to know the way to the Palace?" "No," said the stranger, "I don't," and left him there.'

To the King this seemed such a delightfully silly joke that it was some minutes before he could recover his gravity, but the Princess could only look sadly and wistfully at Count Rollo.

'Well, well,' said the King, 'you shall have one more turn later. Now it is for Count Hoppo to try.'

Now Count Hoppo was minded to try a trick with which he had often amused members of his own family. For it had long been a habit of his, when some unwelcome guest was arriving at his father's door, to prepare a butter-slide in the hall, so that treading unwarily upon it, the visitor should slip, and his feet should fly into the air, and he should fall heavily to the ground, to the great enjoyment of those of the family who were looking on. So for this occasion he had prepared a most amusing butter-slide a few paces from where he and Count Rollo stood, and had warned his father, the Chancellor, to take care that no members of the court trod upon it before the trial began. So now he stepped forward, feeling well assured that in one and the same moment he could win the hand of the Princess and put to shame and laughter the hated Count Rollo.

'I propose,' he said, 'to show Your Royal Highness a small humorous joke of a practical nature, which cannot fail to move Your Royal Highness to loud and hearty laughter. Perhaps, before I begin, the Count Rollo would oblige me by moving a little farther away, so as to give me more room for my joke.' He turned to Rollo. 'If you would be so good as to withdraw a few paces towards the window—'

He indicated with a careless gesture the necessary direction, and bowed to Rollo. Rollo bowed to him in reply; bowed gracefully to the King and still more gracefully to the Princess. Then, still bowing with the utmost ease and elegance, he retired a few paces backwards and stepped gracefully upon the butter-slide.

There was a loud crash.

'Oh!' gasped the Princess. 'Oh-ho-ho-ho-ho-ho! Ha-ha-ha-ha-ha-ha! Oh-he-he-he-he-he!' It was as if somebody had suddenly pressed a button inside her. Her laughter pealed round the Palace walls. She laughed up and up and up and up, and she laughed down and down and down and down. She trilled and gurgled and choked, and choked and gurgled and trilled. It seemed that there was no end to her laughter.

The King too was laughing, the Chancellor was laughing. Count Hoppo was laughing. Save for one man the whole Court was laughing.

Count Rollo did not laugh. Feeling ashamed and miserable and angry, he picked himself up and gave the Princess one reproachful look.

'I'm sorry,' gasped the Princess. 'I didn't mean to laugh, I don't know why I laughed, I don't want to laugh, I . . .' And then she trilled and gurgled and choked, and choked and gurgled and trilled all over again. As soon as quiet was restored, the Chancellor stepped forward.

'Your Majesty,' he said, 'on behalf of the young Count Hoppo, I claim the promised reward.'

'Count Hoppo?' said the King in surprise. 'But it was just an accident, was it not?'

'Not so, Your Majesty,' replied Hoppo proudly. And he explained how, with great cleverness, he had prepared the butter-slide, and how, with great cunning, he had arranged for Count Rollo to step upon it. And all the Court said, 'Well, well, well!' and 'Fancy that now!' And the King frowned and considered the matter.

'Ah, well, in that case,' said His Majesty, 'you may fairly claim to have succeeded in moving Her Royal

Highness to laughter.'

He turned to Count Rollo. 'You agree that that is so, Count Rollo?'

Rollo looked at the Princess, and she looked back at him and their eyes spoke to each other. As plainly as if she were speaking her eyes cried to him, 'Save me from this Count Hoppo!' And Rollo smiled back at her, and gave a little nod, as if he would say, 'It will be all right,' for an idea had come to him.

So he turned like one in thought, and walked a few paces off. Then, turning again to the King, he said:

'Your Majesty, since I have seen Her Royal Highness day by day, these many days, I have dared to love her. If Your Majesty says now that she is to be wedded to the Count Hoppo, it will be better that I should not look upon her again. But I venture to make this last request of her. I ask her to come down from her throne and say farewell to me here, not as Princess to subject, but as maid to man.'

And he went down on one knee and waited for her.

'I will come,' said the Princess softly.

So she came to him; and, as she drew near, she stepped suddenly upon the butter-slide, and her feet shot into the air, and she fell heavily upon the floor.

There was a cry of anger from the Princess, followed by a cry of horror from all the Court. A dozen hands helped her to her feet, and supported her again to the side of her father, who comforted her with Royal Words.

'But this is passing strange,' said Rollo loudly. 'How comes it that Her Royal Highness does not laugh? Was it not a funny jest?'

The King looked at him with suspicion.

'What does this mean?' said the King sternly. 'This talk of saying farewell, was it just a plot to make Her Royal Highness fall?'

'Certainly, Your Majesty,' said Rollo pleasantly. 'I hoped that Count Hoppo's delightful jest would amuse us all again.' He turned to the Princess. 'Was Your Royal Highness not amused?'

'We were not amused,' said Her Royal Highness coldly.

'Certainly not,' said the King with dignity.

'But Your Royal Highness was amused before,' said Rollo gently.

'That was different altogether,' said the King.

Then Count Rollo smiled at them all. 'In that case, Your Majesty, it was not Count Hoppo's butter-slide which made Her Royal Highness laugh, but my extremely humorous way of kicking my feet in the air and falling to the ground.'

Then it was the turn of the Princess to smile, as she saw

what Rollo would be at.

'Why, yes,' said the King in surprise. 'That had not occurred to me, but indeed it would seem to be so. What do you say, my dear?'

'Of course, it is, Father,' said the Princess quickly. 'It was Count Rollo who made me laugh, not Count Hoppo.'

But now Count Hoppo, seeing how things were going against him, cried out suddenly: 'It was me, Your Majesty, it was me! If I had fallen down, I would have made the Princess laugh, just as loudly as Count Rollo did! I'll make her laugh now! Watch me!' And with these words, he ran across the butter-slide so swiftly that his feet leapt in the air, and he shot heavily through the window and dropped twenty feet below, splash! into the Royal Fishpond!

'How vulgar!' said the Princess, with her nose in the air. So young Count Rollo married the Princess, and they lived and loved and laughed happily together for more years than I can remember. But what happened to Count Hoppo when they had dragged him out of the fishpond, I never heard; nor, indeed, does it matter very much.